"Come sit, my child," said the old man
to his grandchild, "and I will tell you the story
of a kiss. There are many sorts of kisses—some
are like feathers, others are snowflakes
and others, leaves . . ."

To kisses of all colors and
countries from whomever they're sent
to whomever they're given
—M. B. and T. V.

Printed in Hong Kong

MARCIAL BÓO

The Butterfly Kiss

Illustrated by Tim Vyner

HARCOURT BRACE & COMPANY   San Diego   New York   London

ONCE THERE WAS a beautiful butterfly kiss which fluttered among the trees of the forest. But the butterfly kiss was not happy.

"My family and friends have found homes," it said, "and now I'm all alone. I wonder if anyone wants me?"

The kiss floated off through the trees to try
to find a home. It drifted past a sleepy-looking
tiger lying on a rock in the shade of a tall tree.
"Would you like a kiss?" it asked the tiger.

"Not just now," said the tiger. "I'm settling down for my morning nap. I'm far too sleepy to kiss anyone."

"Oh, dear," said the kiss. "I'll have to find my home somewhere else."

"Good luck," yawned the tiger.

The kiss darted away from the trees. It flew down to a fat elephant, who was splashing around on the bank of a river.

"Would you like a kiss?" it asked the elephant.

"No, thank you," said the elephant. "I've lots and lots of kisses stored up in my trunk, and I don't need any more at the moment."

"Oh, dear," said the kiss. "I'll have to find my home somewhere else."

"Good-bye," trumpeted the elephant.

The kiss blew away from the riverbank and swept up to the top of a high tree, where a stork had built a nest.

"Would you like a kiss?" it asked the stork.

"Not yet," said the stork. "I'm sitting on my eggs, but they won't hatch for another few days. I won't need any kisses until then."

"Oh, dear," said the kiss. "I'll have to find my home somewhere else."

"See you soon," whistled the stork.

Away wafted the kiss. It soared across the river to a crocodile, who was basking on some mudflats.

"Would you like a kiss?" it asked the crocodile.

"Not likely," said the crocodile. "I don't like kisses. I just snap, snap, snap with my mighty jaws. I don't like kisses at all."

"Oh, dear," said the kiss. "I'll have to find my home somewhere else."

"And don't come back!" gnashed the crocodile.

The kiss swerved quickly away from the crocodile and skimmed into the long grass nearby, where a hare was hiding.

"Would you like a kiss?" it asked the hare.

"I'm afraid not," said the hare. "Hares don't kiss. When we like someone very much, we wiggle our noses up and down and rub them together."

"Oh, dear," said the kiss. "I'll have to find my home somewhere else."

"Farewell," twitched the hare.

The kiss glided away over the fields. It flitted up to the branches of a tree, where a bat was hanging.

"Would you like a kiss?" it asked the bat.

"I don't think so," said the bat. "The sun is going down and I just woke up. I won't need any kisses until my bedtime in the morning."

"Oh, dear," said the kiss. "I'll have to find my home somewhere else."

"Good evening to you," twittered the bat.

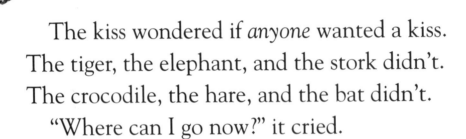

The kiss wondered if *anyone* wanted a kiss.
The tiger, the elephant, and the stork didn't.
The crocodile, the hare, and the bat didn't.

"Where can I go now?" it cried.

"Try over there," said a white cow with large
horns, who was ambling slowly into the village.
Not far away, the kiss saw a light in a window.

The kiss floated through the window. Inside the room was an old man who was telling a story to a child.

"Would you like a kiss?" the kiss asked the child.

"Yes, please," said the child. "Yes! Yes! Yes!"

So the kiss fluttered happily between the old man and his grandchild as they gave each other a goodnight kiss.

First published in Great Britain 1995 by Victor Gollancz
Text copyright © Marcial Bóo 1995
Illustrations copyright © Tim Vyner 1995

First U.S. edition 1995

Library of Congress Cataloging-in-Publication Data
Bóo, Marcial.
The butterfly kiss/Marcial Bóo; illustrated by Tim Vyner.—1st U.S. ed.
p.   cm.
Summary: A butterfly kiss that is not wanted by a tiger,
an elephant, a stork, a crocodile, a hare, or a bat finds a home
where an old man says goodnight to his grandchild.
ISBN 0-15-200841-1
[l. Kissing—Fiction. 2. Butterflies—Fiction. 3. Animals—Fiction.]
I. Vyner, Tim, ill. II. Title.
PZ7.B6448Bu   1995
[E]—dc20   94-41940

A B C D E